KU-656-327

One Special Sleepover

M Christina Butler • Tina Macnaughton

LITTLE TIGER PRESS
London

Little Hedgehog was bustling round his brand new tree house. He was having his first ever sleepover and he couldn't wait for his friends to arrive.

"Anyone at home?" called Badger.

"Come on up!" laughed Little Hedgehog excitedly.

"Oh, this is lovely!" Rabbit gasped as the friends climbed up.

"We brought you a present!" said Mouse. "It's a book of bedtime stories."

"Thank you," smiled Little Hedgehog. "And I've got a present for you. Look!"

"Taa-daah!" cheered Little Hedgehog,
pulling out a colourful, cosy blanket.
"I made it specially! And it's big enough
for all of us to snuggle under."

But as Little Hedgehog shook out the blanket, a gust of wind blew it up into the air and over the treetops!

"Oh no!" cried Little Hedgehog.

"Quick!" yelled Fox, scrambling down the ladder. "Follow that blanket!"

"The wind's blowing it towards the river!" puffed Badger.

But by the time they reached the riverbank the blanket had flopped into the water and was floating away.

"What are we going to do?" sniffed
Little Hedgehog. "We can't have
a sleepover without a blanket!"
"Don't be sad," said Badger.
"Why don't we try and make
a new one?"
"That's a wonderful idea,
Badger!" smiled Little Hedgehog.

And they all scurried off to
look for snippets of cloth.

"Look, Little Hedgehog!" said
Badger as the friends shared
the things they'd found.
"You slept on this cushion
cover after the Big Storm
blew your house away."

"Oh yes, I remember," sighed Little Hedgehog. "You were so kind, and I was so cosy and warm in front of your fire."

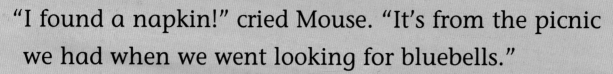

"I found a napkin!" cried Mouse. "It's from the picnic
we had when we went looking for bluebells."

"Poor Mouse!" said Little Hedgehog, shaking
his head. "That was the day you fell down
that deep, dark hole."

"I know," giggled Mouse. "I'd still
be there if you hadn't
pulled me out!"

"Can this go in our blanket?" squeaked
a baby mouse, snuggling into a piece
of cloth covered with stars.
"Of course," smiled Little Hedgehog.
"Does it remind you of anything?"

"Yes!" cried the babies. "When we went to watch the shooting stars!"

"That was such a special night," added Mouse as the friends snipped, sewed and shared their stories together.

In no time at all the blanket was finished.

"Every patch and stitch will remind us of the happy times we've spent together," said Little Hedgehog. "Let's call it our Friendship Blanket!"

"What a lovely idea!" said Badger. "That's just what it is, and we've all helped to make it."

"Hurrah!" they cheered, shaking
out their wonderful blanket.
But Rabbit gasped as a
baby mouse peeped
through a hole in
the middle. "Oh
dear! We need
more cloth!"

"But I've got nothing left!"
cried Little Hedgehog sadly.
"I used all my material to
make the first blanket!"

Suddenly, the two little birds
flew in carrying a piece of
bright red cloth.

"It's from your lost blanket,
Little Hedgehog!" cried Fox.
"They must have found it
near the river."

"Oh, thank you!" called
Little Hedgehog. "It'll fit
perfectly."

Little Hedgehog's needle flashed in the lantern light as he stitched the very last square into place.

"Now there's a patchwork piece from all of us!" he cried and all his friends cheered.

The woods grew dark and the tree house swayed gently in the night wind. Everyone snuggled beneath the blanket as Badger read a story.

"All my friends together," Little Hedgehog whispered happily. "What a perfect sleepover!"

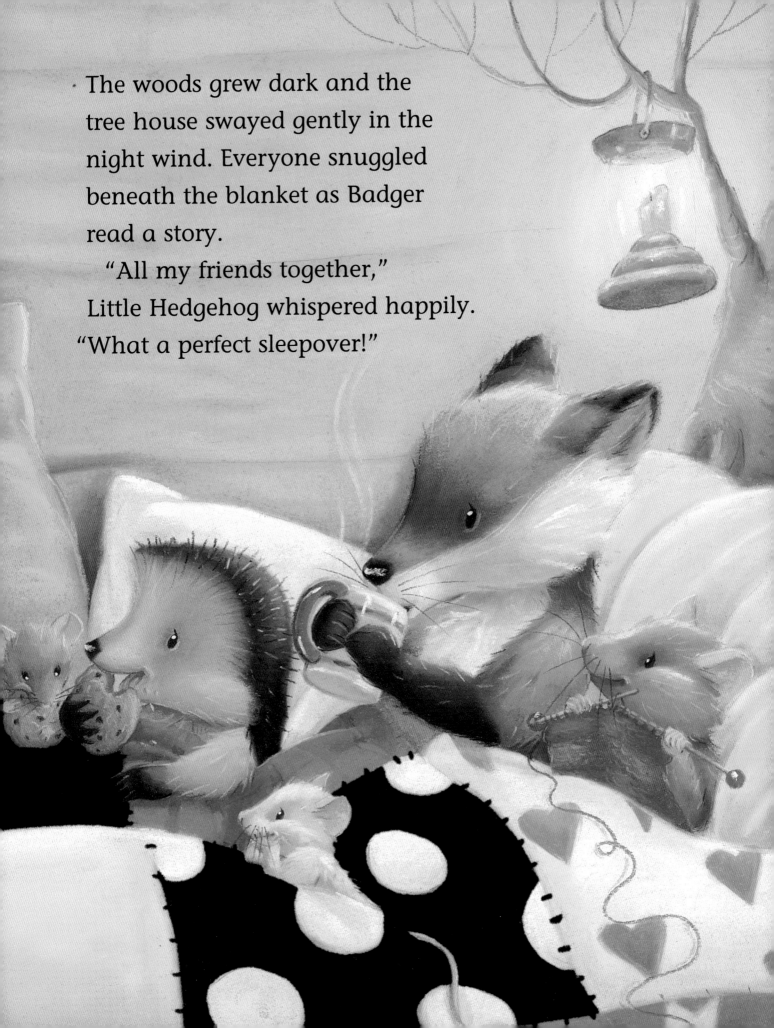

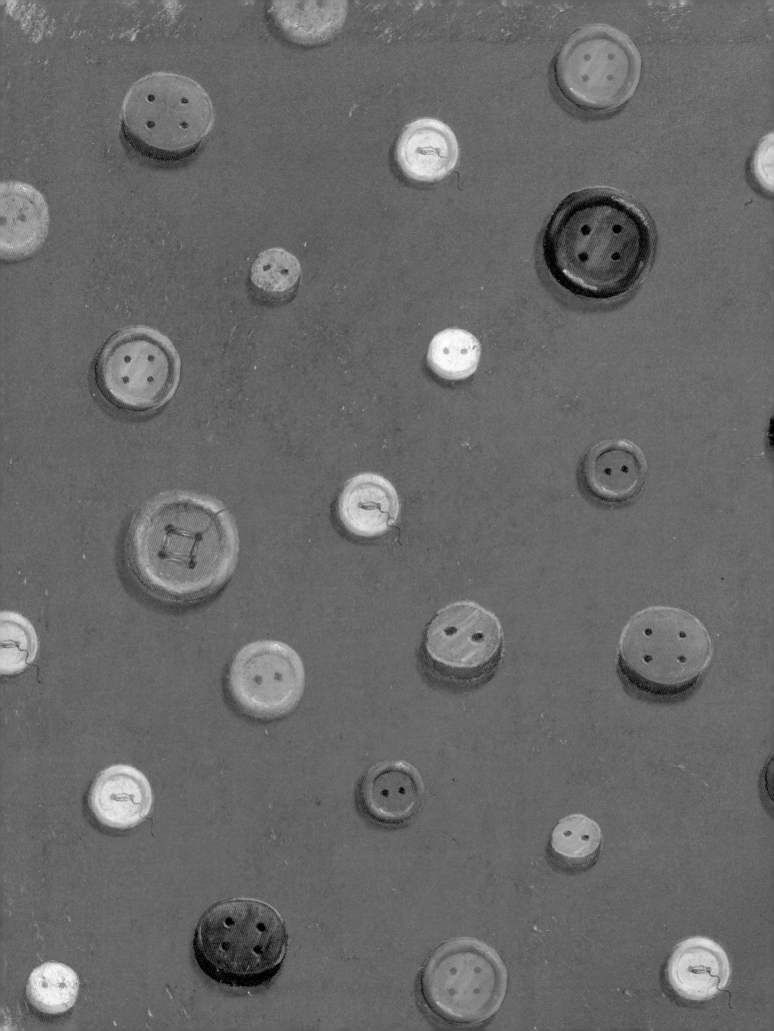